Little Greeter

A Grunion Tale

Authored By:

Eileen Ryan McMillen

ACKNOWLEDGMENTS

Seeing this project to completion took the collaboration of many people. First and foremost, I would like to thank my son, Ryan McMillen, for this technical assistance throughout the publishing and illustrating process. Without his help, this project would not have come to fruition. Appreciation goes to our illustrator, Ricky, who did a fantastic job of capturing the nighttime grunion scenes.

Pepperdine University deserves recognition for giving my husband, Bill, and I the opportunity to be Grunion Greeters at Goleta State Beach, CA in 2009. I am grateful for my family for the inspiration for the characters and for their love and especially to Bill for his support through this project and my life. Lastly, great admiration goes to Mother Nature for creating such an interesting and dazzling world where fish come ashore to twirl around on the beach, as if in a nighttime dance off!

Long after dark, Mom and Dad gathered the three of us: my older sister and brother, and me, to go to the beach.

"Why the beach at night?", I asked. "There might be a party," Dad replied.

We grabbed jackets against the chill and flashlights for the dark.

By the time we arrived, however, the moon had climbed to the top of the sky. We could see our favorite beach from the highway. If there was a party here, there was no bonfire and no picnic. It was still.

As we headed down toward the wet sand, I wanted to use my flashlight, but my sister said to use only the moon for now.

She and my brother had been to this party before.

They knew.

The noise of the highway disappeared and only the crashing sound of the waves remained.

The white water glistened in the golden glow as it rushed on shore.

It was a high tide this night in spring.

The five of us wandered slowly down the sloping sand toward the pier. I had lots of questions, but for now, we were silent.

The parents said we were hoping to welcome special guests who were a little shy. These guests did not like loud noises or bright lights.

I knew about shy. So I kept my flashlight off and held my questions inside.

We wandered on and passed a few others who were equally silent.

They greeted us with nods and we did the same, but no words were spoken.

There was a feeling of anticipation all around.

I became lost in the sounds and shadows.

My sandled toes grew cold in the wet sand and water.

Before I could voice my concern to my mother, we came upon another beach goer.

There in the shallows stood a tall, slender egret, silent and still.

His sliver white body shimmered and pulsed in the moonlight.

He stared. We stared, then tiptoed past.

Further down the shore, the whispered shout of my brother could be heard.

"Scouts, scouts!"

I looked that way.

Several small silvery fish had ridden in on a wave.

They flipped and they flopped and twinkled like stars.

Dad told me they were grunion. They were unique to our area. That's why this was a special party.

The scouts are boy grunion called males. They come ashore first to see if this beach is a good place to gather. If it is, the scouts go back out to sea and call the others.

Several more scouts came in on the next couple waves and quickly returned. "Now we wait", Dad said softly.

We moved to the shadow of a palm tree so not to disturb the grunion. I bounced from foot to foot hoping the little visitors would come. I wanted to welcome the grunion.

To ease the wait, I counted waves. "One, two", when I reached sixteen, suddenly the shore was aglow with dozens of glittery, wiggly grunion.

Dad said, "These are the girls, the females. Watch what they do!"

As I watched in quiet expectation, the females twirled their tail fins and slowly dug a hole for themselves.

They continued until only their heads showed.

"They're laying eggs", Mom told me.

Male grunion surfed in on the next couple waves, so many, the sand was hidden.

They circled and danced and danced around the females to music only they could hear.

Maybe they were excited to be dads I thought.

When the dancing was through, the males caught the next several waves back to sea.

The females also rode out on the next few waves.

Shortly, the shore was empty.

The special party, called a grunion run, was over.

Quiet fell like a blanket over us as we headed back the way we came.

"Can we come again?", I asked.

"Next high tide in two weeks", my Mom said. "But remember, when you go to a grunion run, the grunion may come, or the grunion may not".

Then, from somewhere behind us came a loud "Whoop! Whoop!" as my brother twirled and danced down the beach like a grunion.

I watched and as I often do, I followed filled with giddiness from being a greeter at a grunion run.

Information Page

Mother Nature created both a mystery and a miracle with the birth of the tiny grunion. The only time the five to six-inch slender fish are seen is during spawning season from April through August and only on the sandy beaches from Southern California to Baja.

They come ashore on the three nights following the highest tide of the full and the new moon. It is always around midnight when they appear.

The eggs usually wait ten days to two weeks to hatch at the next high tide. When they are one year old, the grunion are ready for their own spawning ritual.

Harvesting the grunion is limited to bare hand catching only and not during peak spawning months of April and May.
Climate changes and destruction of habitat, mainly from development, have led to a decline in grunion population. For this reason, I recommend a catch and release or observation policy only. For more information visit: grunion.pepperdine.edu

ABOUT THE AUTHOR

Eileen McMillen is a former school teacher with a master's degree in education. She lives with her husband Bill in the sunny Santa Ynez Valley of California where they raised their three children. They enjoy their active vegan lifestyle that includes long swims in the ocean, creating flavorful nutritious plant-based meals, and walking their rescue pup Abbi. After a lifetime of reading to children and spending summers along the California coast with her family, *The Little Greeter, A Grunion Tale*, is this educator's foray into the publishing world.

Made in the USA
Columbia, SC
22 May 2018